OVER BACK

by Beverly Major • illustrated by Thomas B. Allen

HarperCollins*Publishers*

OVER BACK

Library of Congress Cataloging-in-Publication Data
Major, Beverly.
    Over Back / by Beverly Major ; illustrated by Thomas B. Allen.
        p.   cm.
    Summary: A young girl's favorite spot is Over Back, a place of
pools and trees over across the fields back behind the barn, where
the wonders of nature wait to be discovered each day.
    ISBN 0-06-020286-6. — ISBN 0-06-020287-4 (lib. bdg.)
    [1. Country life—Fiction.   2. Nature—Fiction.]   I. Allen,
Thomas B., ill.   II. Title.
PZ7.M27990v   1993   91-19696
[E]—dc20   CIP
                                                                          AC

For Ruth Curran,

who has been Over Back
—B.M.

To the preservation

of Walden Woods
—T.B.A.

Over Back you can pick the best blueberries—the bushes are shiny green, and the purply-blue berries hang heavy on the branches. Over Back you can find big, fat puffballs that spurt smoky clouds when you step on them. Over Back there are stones that you can use like chalk—stones that write in red and yellow and blue. Over Back means "over across the fields, back behind the barn." But nobody has to say that. We just say "Over Back."

Over Back is where you go with your brother or your sister or your cousin or your friend—a real friend or a make-believe one. Mothers never go there, so while you're Over Back, they can't tell you not to get dirty and not to wade in the creek and not to pick up rocks because they might have snakes underneath them.

Here's how you get there—Over Back. You go behind the barn, and you follow the dirt road that the hay wagons have made. It winds and twists through three hay fields. Then you come to the stone wall. There's a kind of gate made of wire to keep the cows in the next field, but you don't use the gate. You climb up the wall and jump over the side. You have to be careful to place your feet firmly when you jump. If you're not careful, the stones in the wall will growl at you with a scraping sound, and they'll move under your feet, and you'll twist your ankle when you land.

But you jump just right, and land flat on your feet, ready to cross the pasture field. The cows come here to find the sweetest, greenest grass. You walk through this field. The cows swing their big heads up to look at

you, and some might move a couple of steps,
but mostly they just stare awhile and then they
bend to eat some more. Cows have beautiful
long eyelashes, did you know?

Now there's another kind of field where, when you're lucky, you'll find secrets. No long, lush grass, but hummocks and huge rocks scattered as if a giant had thrown a handful of pebbles. The hummocks are mossy. In the spring, down under the moss you can find wintergreen berries, bright red with spongy white insides. When you chew the berries or the tender little red leaves, your mouth feels clean and new and minty.

And arbutus. Down under the moss are the small, pale-pink flowers, like little new stars that have been wakened from a nap. They have the sweetest smell in the world. Finding arbutus is like finding a treasure. You have to smell the flowers and smell them again, the way you have to keep looking at a rainbow until it's gone.

It's hard to tell where Over Back begins. Maybe it begins with the arbutus. Or with the bridge. There's a bridge over a creek. The bridge was made a hundred years ago. It's just big rocks thrown into the creek, the way you make a dam; on top of the rocks, there's dirt, to make the road. The bridge belongs to Over Back. No cars go across it, only hay wagons pulled by the big steamy horses, Bob White and Jim, and sometimes the little tractor dragging a plow. It's a private bridge.

The water in the creek has found a path under the rocks, so that the creek can go on, but the bridge makes the water hesitate and form a pool. The pool is a slow and silver place. The water is green and blue and silver. Dragonflies, looking long and dangerous with silver and purple glinting off their wings, buzz and sway over the water's surface. Along the edges of the pool are globs of frogs' eggs, silvery too, reflecting the blue and green of the water. When you pick them up, they feel like Jell-O in your hand, and they move and shift like Jell-O too. Inside each egg is a tiny black sliver—a baby frog waiting to be born.

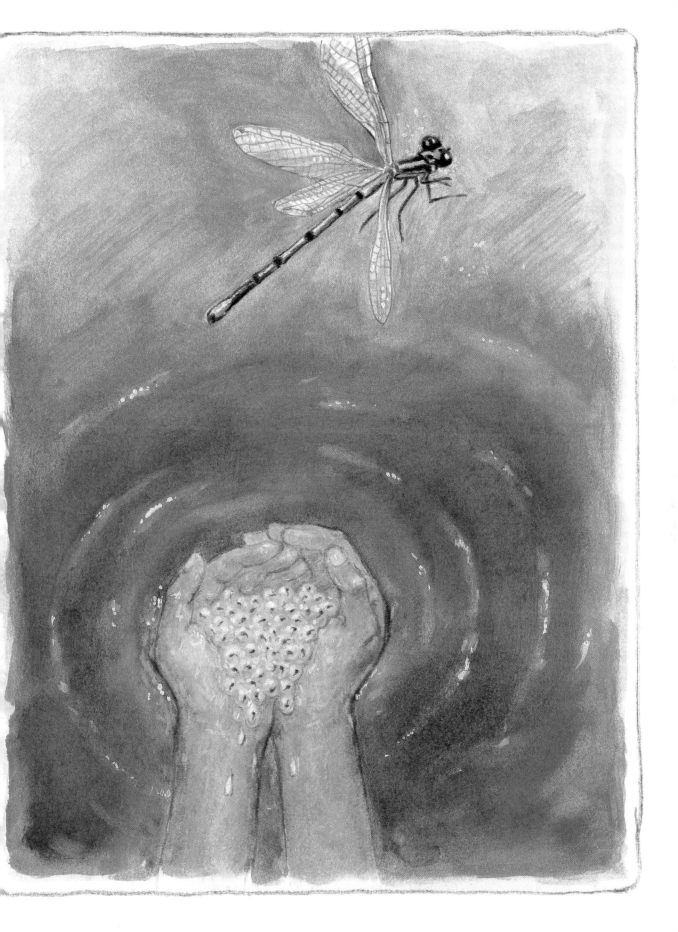

If you follow the creek beyond the bridge, you'll find another pool—just a widening in the creek, really—under the shade of a huge pine tree. The water here is shallow and clear; you can watch minnows darting beneath its surface, their shadows on the rocky creek bottom much larger than they are. Are they afraid of their shadows?

Sometimes it's nice to wade in the creek. You can find salamanders under rocks along the bank, tiny monsters of the brightest shiny black with red or yellow spots, so shiny that they look as though they had a light inside them. Don't take them away with you. They'll get homesick for their creek; their colors will dim, the shine will leave their skin, and sadness will take their light away.

Sometimes you'll find a toad, all rough and warty-looking like a tree root. If you hold him gently in your hand, you can watch the pulsing of his throat. His stomach feels as soft as velvet.

There's a whole field of pine trees Over Back. They're so close together that nothing else grows in this field. Just the pine trees whispering over a carpet of soft brown needles, like a blanket covering their toes. It is so quiet, you want to hold somebody's hand. Deer sleep there, on the brown blanket. Last year in almost winter I stood on the edge of the pine grove and watched the deer get up and stretch themselves. They stood like cutout silhouettes on the edge of the grove against a rosy sunset sky—and then they ran away, leaping and twisting without a sound, as light as milkweed-down blown in the wind.

When the sun begins to slide down in the sky, you can hear from far away, drifting on the air, "Cow boss, cow boss." Except it sounds like *cuh-boss, cuh-boss.* That's someone calling the cows to come home. Some have already begun to wander toward the lane that leads to the barn, but very slowly, stopping every few steps to take a bite of grass. You can hurry them up a little. You run in a kind of half circle behind them, and you yell, "Hey, cow. Move, cow." And finally they all begin to move, slowly, from front to back, like a wave building.

The lane that leads to the barn is trapped between stone walls. At the lane's entrance is a spring where the cows gather for a long drink before the last leg home. The water gushes from an old rusty pipe into a wooden box, green with moss. The cows lower their noses into the water and slurp. You can hear them swallow, *ga-lung, ga-lung.*

Sometimes you take a drink too. You flop on your stomach, and you catch the water as it comes from the pipe, in your mouth, on your nose, down your chin, icy, icy, so cold it feels like a solid thing.

And then you know it's dinnertime, and you're hungry and you're tired, tired, tired, and your legs ache, and the lane stretches up the hill, and the barn is far away.

So you run ahead of the cows. You climb on the stone wall that borders the lane and you wait for Ginger, the dusty brown cow. You wait as coiled and ready as a grasshopper, as ready as a cowboy at the rodeo. When Ginger moves past your spot, you spring up and forward and throw yourself onto her back! Her back is bony and slippery, and if you've jumped too hard, you'll slide right off the other side. But if you jump just right, you're suddenly up above the world, like an Indian princess on an elephant. You hold on tight with your knees; you bend forward and lay your cheek on the coarse hair of Ginger's neck and shut your eyes. You can feel the way her body moves, slow and lumpy, bumpy, one part after the other, not all at once and smoothly like a horse.

And then you're at the barn. You slide off Ginger's back before she goes in the barn door because it's a narrow door, and she might pinch your leg against the frame. You just swing both legs to the same side and slide off like you slide down a sliding board. You hit the ground with a thump. Your legs are stiff, and your bones remember the jerk and sway of a ride on a cow; for a little while you feel as though you're still riding.

And then you hear your mother calling "Dinnertime." Just for a second, you stand behind the barn at the top of the lane. You look toward Over Back and there it is, waiting for tomorrow.